D1520442

UNICEF

Deborah A. Grahame

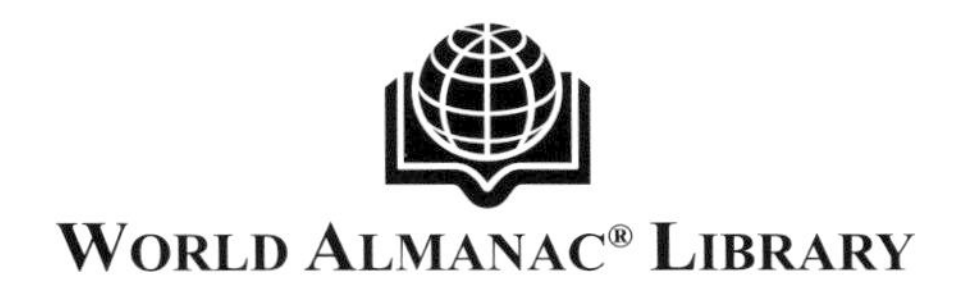

Please visit our web site at: www.worldalmanaclibrary.com
For a free color catalog describing World Almanac® Library's list
of high-quality books and multimedia programs, call 1-800-848-2928 (USA)
or 1-800-387-3178 (Canada). World Almanac® Library's fax: (414) 332-3567.

Library of Congress Cataloging-in-Publication Data

Grahame, Deborah A.
UNICEF/ by Deborah A. Grahame.
p. cm. — (International organizations)
Includes bibliographical references and index.
Contents: Heed the suffering of children — Health, hunger, and HIV — The task of education — Women and girls — Children in difficulty — A new century for children.
ISBN 0-8368-5522-1 (lib. bdg.)
ISBN 0-8368-5531-0 (softcover)
1. UNICEF —Juvenile literature. [1. UNICEF.] I. Title. II. International organizations (Milwaukee, Wis.)
HV703.G72 2003
362.7—dc21 2003045036

First published in 2004 by
World Almanac® Library
330 West Olive Street, Suite 100
Milwaukee, WI 53212 USA

Developed by Books Two, Inc.
Editor: Jean B. Black
Design and Maps: Krueger Graphics, Inc.: Karla J. Krueger and Victoria L. Buck
Indexer: Chandelle Black
World Almanac® Library editor: JoAnn Early Macken
World Almanac® Library art direction: Tammy Gruenewald

Photo Credits: Courtesy UNICEF: logo, HQ97-0564/Photographer Unknown, HQ00-0474/Radhika Chalasani 16, HQ98-0028/Stuart Freedman 27, HQ02-0053/Roger LeMoyne 8, HQ02-0039/Roger LeMoyne 25, DHQ100/Susan Markisz 40, HQ02-0126/Susan Markisz 42, HQ01-0309/Shafqat Munir 14, HQ01-0292/Shehzad Noorani 31, HQ01-0181/Giacomo Pirozzi 20, HQ92-0940/Nicole Toutonji 7, HQ91-0241/Nicole Toutonji 43; © CICR/DUTOIT, Philippe: 36; © Howard Davies/CORBIS: 34; © Louise Gubb/CORBIS: 21; © IFRC/Black, Christopher: 17; © David Turnley/CORBIS: 38; © Peter Turnley/CORBIS: 18; United Nations Photo Library: cover, 5, 10, 11, 24, 28, 33, © WHO/photo: 12; © WHO/P. VIROT: 13, 15, 22, 38

Printed in the United States of America

1 2 3 4 5 6 7 8 9 07 06 05 04 03

TABLE OF CONTENTS

Words that appear in the glossary are printed in **boldface** type the first time they occur in the text.

Chapter One Heed the Suffering of Children

It is early morning in a village in Afghanistan. People are already at prayer in the local place of worship, or **mosque**. A voice makes an announcement over the mosque loudspeakers. "Free measles **vaccines** today! Come to the mosque with your children now!" The message blasts throughout the village. The line outside the mosque grows long quickly. Some children become frightened as the time for their vaccinations draws near. Mothers, fathers, and grandparents do their best to encourage the children to be brave. Inside, a team of public health workers is busy. A needle jabs quickly into another child's arm. Those just outside the vaccination room can hear the child wail. In response, several children still waiting their turn start to cry. Soon, more children in line hear the crying and join in.

These children in a Mayan village in South America were vaccinated by a visiting health care volunteer.

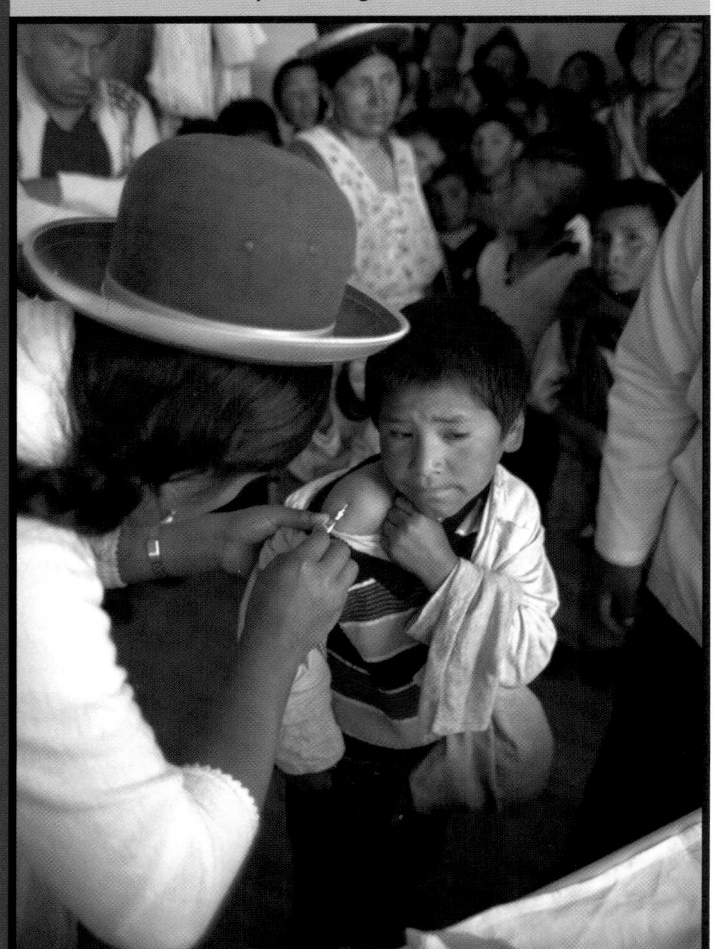

The adults waiting in line are happy, however. In the past, many children in Afghanistan died because they were not **immunized** against measles, the nation's number one killer. In 2002, most Afghan children between the ages of six months and twelve years were immunized. To make this happen, local officials in Afghanistan worked with an international agency called UNICEF, the United Nations Children's Fund.

The Cause of Children

Afghanistan is just one small country, and vaccinating children is only the beginning of the work UNICEF does. The organization helps children in 158 countries and territories in several key ways. These include health care and nutrition, safe water and sanitation, basic education, protection of mothers and infants, and protection of children in difficulty.

UNICEF summarizes its mission this way: "To promote the survival, protection, and development of all children worldwide." The organization has emphasized two of its goals—"Health for All" and "Water and Sanitation for All."

Children in post-World War II Europe asked for milk.

How UNICEF Began

UNICEF was started in response to the suffering of children caused by a terrible war. War destroys much more than buildings, airplanes, and ships. War destroys lives. Children who survive wars often have lost families, friends, and homes. They also may have lost a good way of life and hope for a happy future. No one is hurt more by the horror of war than children.

World War II (1939-1945) was fought in Europe, the Middle East, and the Pacific. About fifty million people died. The war left great destruction in many countries. Leaders of the world wanted to be sure this kind of war never happened again. They began to call for the creation of a single peacekeeping organization made up of many nations.

Several important gatherings of world leaders took place. The result was the formation of the United Nations (UN) in 1945. The UN realized that children in Europe were suffering terribly after the war. The children did not have enough food, medicine, or clothing. Winter had begun, and there was a lack of shelter and fuel for warmth. The war had ended, but children still suffered from its effects. Worst of all, many children, especially babies, were dying of disease and starvation.

In response to this emergency, the United Nations created a special agency for children. It was first known as the International Children's Emergency Fund, or ICEF. The fund provided children in Europe with a simple but important food product—dried milk. Other forms of aid, such as vaccinations against tuberculosis (TB), were also given.

An important feature about this relief is that it was offered to all children in crisis equally. It did not matter whether their country had been on the winning or losing side of the war. This equality is still at the core of UNICEF's response to children in need around the world. In 1953, the ICEF became a permanent part of the United Nations. Its official name became United Nations Children's Fund, but it is still called UNICEF.

The Founder of UNICEF

Dr. Ludwik Rajchman of Poland (1881–1965) refused to see the good work of ICEF end after the ending of World War II. He wanted the agency to continue helping children. He wanted it to work on the problems of poverty and disease throughout the world. As a delegate at a meeting in Geneva, he spoke out forcefully. UN member nations and nations emerging after the war joined his cause. On December 11, 1946, the UN General Assembly created what would become UNICEF. In 1953, the UN General Assembly passed a resolution to continue the work for children.

In the beginning, UNICEF's main goal was to feed children in areas that had been destroyed during World War II. But thanks to the vision of people like Dr. Rajchman, its function continued to grow.

The Declaration

In 1959, the UN General Assembly adopted a document that expresses the ideas and beliefs held by UNICEF. The document is called the Declaration of the Rights of the Child. Here are some of the important phrases:

The child shall enjoy special protection . . . to enable him to develop physically, mentally, morally, spiritually, and socially in a healthy and normal manner and in conditions of freedom and dignity. (From Principle 2)

The child shall be entitled from his birth to a name and a nationality. (From Principle 3)

The child shall have the right to adequate nutrition, housing, recreation, and medical services. (From Principle 4)

The child who is physically, mentally, or socially handicapped shall be given the special treatment, education, and care required by his particular condition. (From Principle 5)

The child, for the full and harmonious development of his personality, needs love and understanding. (From Principle 6)

The child is entitled to receive education. . . . The child shall have full opportunity for play and recreation . . . . (From Principle 7)

The child shall in all circumstances be among the first to receive protection and relief. (From Principle 8)

Where Does the Money Come From?

It takes large sums of money to accomplish UNICEF's goals. Most of UNICEF's money comes from the governments of the UN's member nations as well as nonmember nations. Individual and group donations from around the world are also an importance source of income. UNICEF does not receive funds automatically from UN member nations. All of UNICEF's funds are received on a voluntary basis. This means that people and nations give any amount they wish to and can afford.

In the United States, staff and volunteers of the U.S. Fund for UNICEF are dedicated to reaching UNICEF's goals. They develop special teaching materials and visit schools to talk about ways the organization helps the world's children. They create key partnerships with the private sector and other organizations to further UNICEF's work and encourage members of the U.S. Congress to be **advocates**, or strong supporters, of children's rights. They also raise money by selling UNICEF greeting cards.

The Mission of UNICEF

UNICEF is mandated by the United Nations General Assembly to advocate for the protection of children's rights, to help meet their basic needs, and to expand their opportunities to reach their full potential.

UNICEF is guided by the Convention on the Rights of the Child and strives to establish children's rights as enduring ethical principles and international standards of behavior toward children.

UNICEF insists that the survival, protection, and development of children are universal development **imperatives** that are **integral** to human progress.

UNICEF mobilizes political will and material resources to help countries, particularly developing countries, ensure a "first call for children" and to build their capacity to form appropriate policies and deliver services for children and their families.

UNICEF is committed to ensuring special protection for the most disadvantaged children — victims of war, disasters, extreme poverty, and all forms of violence and exploitation and those with disabilities.

UNICEF responds in emergencies to protect the rights of children. In coordination with United Nations partners and humanitarian agencies, UNICEF makes its unique facilities for rapid response available to its partners to relieve the suffering of children and those who provide their care.

UNICEF is nonpartisan, and its cooperation is free of discrimination. In everything it does, the most disadvantaged children and the countries in greatest need have priority.

UNICEF aims, through its country programs, to promote the equal rights of women and girls and to support their full participation in the political, social, and economic development of their communities.

UNICEF works with all its partners toward the attainment of the **sustainable** human development goals adopted by the world community and the realization of the vision of peace and social progress enshrined in the Charter of the United Nations.

The "Trick-or-Treat for UNICEF" program is one way the U.S. Fund gets many children involved. This method of raising money began on Halloween in 1950. A few children in Philadelphia carried decorated milk cartons door to door to collect coins for poor children in other countries.

Girls from Namibia (left) and the United States dressed for Halloween showed their "Trick-or-Treat for UNICEF" collection boxes. They asked for money for UNICEF instead of candy for themselves.

They raised $17 that year. Since then, generations of trick-or-treaters have collected coins—more than $188 million worth—instead of candy.

In the 1960s, organizations like UNICEF faced new challenges. The world was changing rapidly. Many nations, particularly in Africa, were gaining their independence. They were no longer colonies of larger nations such as Britain and France. These developing nations needed the help of wealthy nations, such as the United States, in business, agriculture, and technology. Most of all, they needed help to overcome poverty and disease. The work of UNICEF had to be broadened to deal with all the new problems.

The UN declared 1979 the International Year of the Child (IYC). The IYC put children first. It addressed difficult problems, such as child abuse and child labor. It opened the way for the passage in 1989 of a new document on child rights, the Convention on the Rights of the Child (CRC). This document lists human rights that are shared by children everywhere. The CRC replaced the 1959 Declaration of the Rights of the Child. UNICEF says it spells out "the basic human rights that children everywhere—without discrimination—have: the right to survival; to develop to the fullest; to protection from harmful influences, abuse and

A Cambodian child waved the United Nations flag during the 1990 World Summit for Children in New York.

exploitation; and to participate fully in family, cultural, and social life."

The World **Summit** for Children took place in September 1990 at UN headquarters. Many world leaders met together—more than ever had before. The Summit led to important changes for children through the plans of action agreed on to reduce disease, **malnutrition**, deaths related to childbirth, and illiteracy. The Convention on the Rights of the Child was passed into international law, giving it great power throughout the world to change the lives of children.

Since 1990, laws reflecting the CRC have been passed in many countries. More than 190 countries have committed themselves to the CRC. The United States was among the last nations to sign the convention, which conveys a commitment, but the U.S. Senate has not yet **ratified** the CRC.

Some legal, religious, and civil groups are concerned that the rights of parents will be weakened. They fear that the government will take away the individual freedom of parents in making decisions regarding their children's welfare. These same groups have also expressed reluctance to subjecting U.S. legal and social systems to UN authority such as that required by the new International Criminal Court.

The Organization

UNICEF is run by its Executive Board, which is made up of thirty-six members who serve three-year terms. Seats on the board are allotted

The Nobel Peace Prize

In 1965, UNICEF was awarded the Nobel Peace Prize. It was accepted by Henry R. Labouisse, the executive director, for Maurice Pate, the long-time head of UNICEF who had died not long before.

In his acceptance speech, Labouisse noted, "The hard reality is that, in more than one hundred developing countries of the world, the odds that confront the average child today—not to say a sickly one—are still overwhelming. They are four to one against his receiving any medical attention, at birth or afterwards. Even if he survives until school age, the chances are two to one that he will get no education at all; if he does get into school, the chances are about four to one that he will not complete the elementary grades. Almost certainly he will have to work for a living by the time he is twelve. He will work to eat—to eat badly and not enough. And his life will, on the average, end in about forty years." UNICEF continues to work to change such a reality.

according to regions: Africa provides eight members, Asia seven, Eastern Europe four, Latin America and the Caribbean five, and Western Europe and other states (including Japan and the United States) twelve. The Executive Board elects its five officers—a president and four vice presidents representing the same five regions.

The Secretariat is the organization that carries out the directions of the Executive Board. It is run by the executive director. The first and longest-serving executive director was Maurice Pate (1946–1965). Nine months after Pate's death, UNICEF received the Nobel Peace Prize. Pate was followed by Henry Labouisse (1965–1979). James P. Grant (1979–1995) was a leader who inspired great change over the years. Since 1995, the executive director has been American attorney and former Peace Corps director Carol Bellamy.

For administrative purposes, UNICEF is divided into seven regions. The Americas and Europe each make up one region. Africa—including the Middle East—has three, and Asia has two.

Chapter Two Health, Hunger, and HIV

Why did UNICEF become involved in health care for children? The answer begins with a bit of history. Disease had spread rapidly throughout Europe during World War II. The war ended in 1945. European people were weakened by the destruction and poverty that remained. Tuberculosis, or TB, continued to threaten people who had survived the war. (TB was known as the "white plague" because of the very pale appearance of its victims.) In 1947, the Scandinavian Red Cross asked the ICEF to help vaccinate all European children against TB. The largest vaccination program ever attempted, this program was the beginning of UNICEF's commitment to children's health.

Victory through Vaccines

During the 1950s, health care experts focused on epidemics, the large-scale spread of disease. These epidemic diseases usually were not related to wars. They spread partly because of poverty and ignorance. The fight against epidemic diseases spread beyond Europe to Asia, Latin America, Africa, and the Middle East.

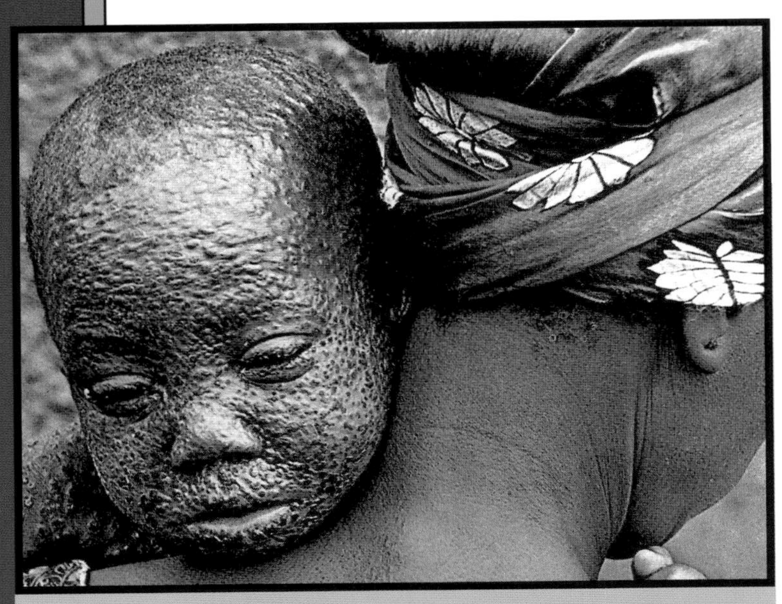

This African baby suffered from smallpox in the days before vaccines became widespread.

It was an exciting time for international health workers. During the twentieth century, new drugs and vaccines had been developed. Penicillin was a miracle cure for many diseases, including TB. Also developed to fight TB was a vaccine known as BCG. More than one million children in post-war Europe received the BCG vaccine during the campaign launched by UNICEF and the Scandinavian Red Cross.

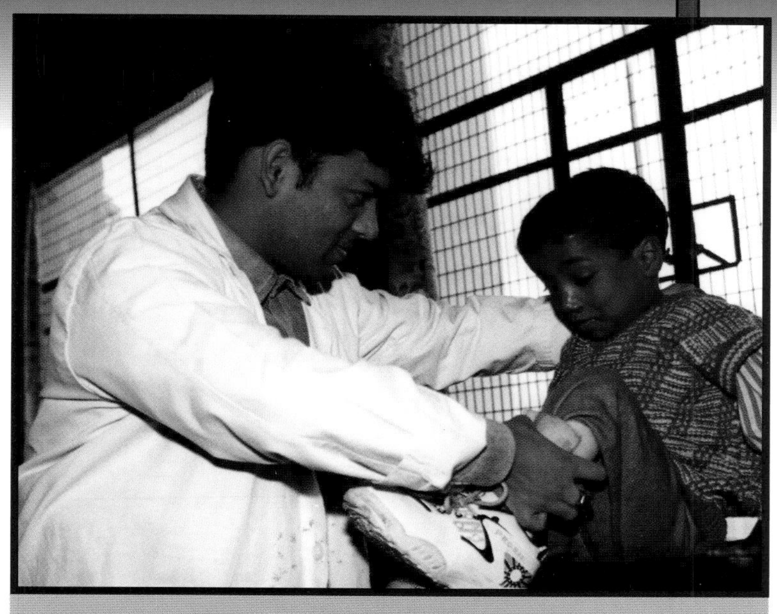

The crippling effects of polio left this child in India wearing leg braces to help him walk.

In Asia and other parts of the world, a condition called yaws was a major concern. Yaws is a contagious, painful skin condition. It affected people in rural and tropical areas during the 1950s. Just one injection of penicillin cleared the victim's skin of ugly pink sores. Yaws was completely cured with just a few more injections. In Thailand and Indonesia, UNICEF helped treat more than one million cases of this disfiguring disease.

Other cures besides penicillin came on the scene during the 1950s. About four hundred million people suffered from an eye infection called trachoma. Health workers gave out an eye ointment to cure it. UNICEF workers also treated leprosy and malaria at this time.

Over the years, UNICEF has supported vaccine programs worldwide, making some areas free of certain diseases. For example, Latin America and the Caribbean have reported no new cases of polio since 1994. China was declared polio-free in 2001. Polio still affects people in Angola and the Democratic Republic of the Congo, however. UNICEF volunteers go door to door in these countries to make sure every child is vaccinated.

In the Middle East and North Africa, the number of polio cases has dropped 90 percent since 1990. In 2001, about 1,350,000 Somali children

Khar Cruisers

When a khar cruiser comes into view, people become excited and spread the word. What's the word? Vaccines! What's a khar cruiser? No, it's not a fancy vehicle. "Khar" means donkey in the Dari language of Afghanistan. Donkeys carry large loads of supplies into villages that are hard to reach by road. Often, there are no roads at all. These animals can make it through tough mountain terrain, even in snow. They go where mechanical vehicles cannot. Health workers walk along with the donkeys. These "khars" are cheaper than cars—they cost only about $10 a day, and they rarely break down. The UNICEF worker shown here is leading a convoy of more than seven hundred pack animals.

were vaccinated. By 2005, UNICEF expects Somalia to be polio-free. In Afghanistan, however, progress is slow because of the conflicts that continue there.

Civil war in Angola ended in April 2002, but UNICEF and other health organizations that worked in Angola during the war continued after the war. Today, malaria is still a big concern. In 2001, more than three million children received polio vaccines. Measles is the number one preventable killer of Angolan children today, killing ten thousand every year. Children who are undernourished are especially vulnerable. In 2003, measles vaccines were given to more than seven million Angolan children, most of the very young population. UNICEF also provides other vaccines, such as those that fight yellow fever and tetanus.

Controlling Malaria?

In the 1950s, DDT spray was used to wipe out the mosquitoes that carry germs causing malaria. At that time, 200 million people died of malaria each year. DDT was often used to spray the walls of houses where mosquitoes bred. DDT use had some problems, however. Nomadic people in countries where malaria was widespread, such as Iran and Thailand, moved around according to the season. They moved their homes with them, and the effect of spraying did not last.

Through the years, there were also shortages of DDT supplies. Use of DDT eventually declined due to health and environmental concerns. The UN is considering a global ban on the use of DDT in 2004. Malaria is on the rise in developing countries, however. Tropical disease specialists from the World Health Organization (WHO), one of UNICEF's partners, have argued that DDT should still be used in these countries, because it is still the most effective weapon against disease-carrying mosquitoes.

In the end, that 1950s UNICEF malaria campaign was unsuccessful. The malaria problem proved to be bigger than mere mosquitoes. The problem involved people's behavior as well as mosquito behavior. UNICEF failed to control either mosquitoes or people for long.

As a result, UNICEF and the worldwide health community learned an important lesson. The health community cannot force health upon people in developing nations. It is necessary to respect the cultures and lifestyles of people in these nations. The people must agree to be part of their own health solutions.

Nutrition

Feeding children has been a top priority for UNICEF since it began. After World War II, UNICEF shipped dried milk to millions of malnourished children throughout Europe. In Africa during the 1950s, malnutrition was widespread. It was considered as dangerous a killer as disease. UNICEF's answer to hunger and lack of nutrition was simple: milk. The

A mother in Somalia carried her two small babies many miles to reach a UNICEF feeding station to prevent them from starving to death.

United States at this time produced more milk than it could use, and it offered groups such as UNICEF the extra milk products for free. UNICEF also helped dairy farmers in poor countries by opening factories for pasteurizing and drying milk.

Not all of UNICEF's efforts to stop hunger have been smooth or successful. In the 1950s and 1960s, UNICEF and other organizations acted on information from a study published in 1952. This study noted that lack of protein was the main cause of malnutrition. The lack of protein was considered a disease, and it even had a strange-sounding name: kwashiorkor. UNICEF worked hard to develop protein-rich food products. UNICEF had food plants in Algeria, Chile, Guatemala, and Indonesia, where foods high in protein, such as soy beans, peanuts, fish, and oil seeds, were ground into special mixtures. The process was expensive. Often, the result tasted terrible.

By the 1970s, nutritionists had learned that lack of protein was not truly the main problem. Poor nutrition was simply a lack of good, nutritious food grown or produced nearby. UNICEF began a program to improve local food supplies. UNICEF workers taught mothers ways to make their children's diets healthier. The mothers learned to raise vegetables and livestock and how to store and cook food safely.

Nutrition: It's More than Food

A full stomach does not always mean a healthy diet. Even when there is plenty of food, children may lack important vitamins and nutrients. They may still die of malnutrition. For example, a child in Vietnam may eat only rice from the age of two months on. The child may not suffer from hunger, but the child's body suffers from poor nutrition. Physical and mental illness may lie ahead for the child.

Vitamin A is a vital vitamin found in liver. People who prefer not to eat liver can get plenty of this vitamin from eggs, fruit, and green leafy vegetables. Many children lack these nutritious foods, however. Without enough vitamin A, they are more likely to pick up infections. They may even get serious eye problems that can cause blindness. UNICEF recognizes the importance of this vitamin. Twice a year, in health centers in many countries, UNICEF workers give a dose of vitamin A to children who are weighed and examined there.

Iodine is another building block of child health. Mothers who get too little iodine can give birth to babies who suffer from mental retardation. Adding iodine to table salt is a low-cost, safe way to correct the problem. In 1995, only 39 percent of China's salt was iodized. By 1999, helped by UNICEF efforts, China reached universal salt iodization, with more than 90 percent of households consuming iodized salt.

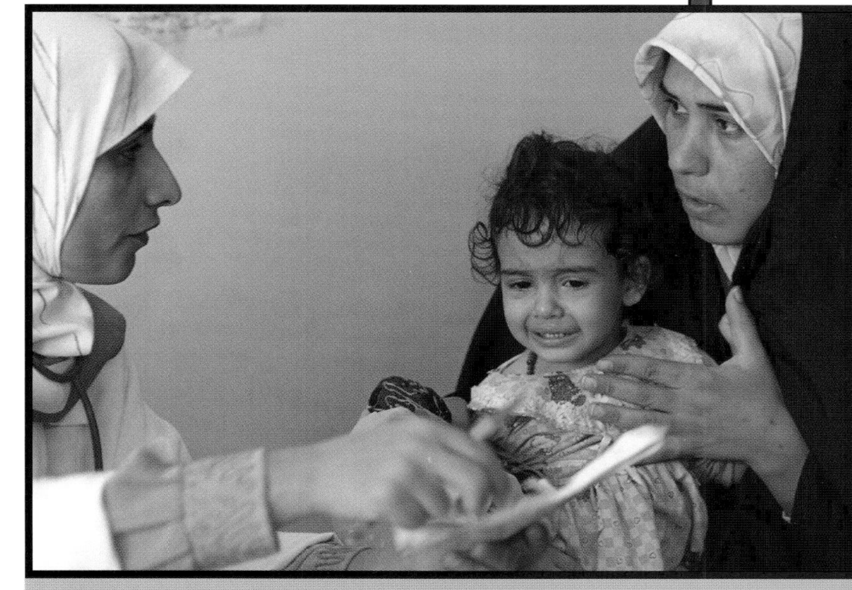

A mother in Iraq brought her child into a UNICEF-supported clinic to be weighed and checked.

Hunger is Happening Today

The image of a starving child is one of the saddest to see. Many people pause for a moment when they see a poster or a TV commercial showing such a child. Then the image fades, and they don't think of it again. Hunger may not seem like such a serious problem, but it is a real one in some parts of the world today.

In Somalia, war keeps food from getting through to half a million starving people. Drought, a long period with no rain, is also a major

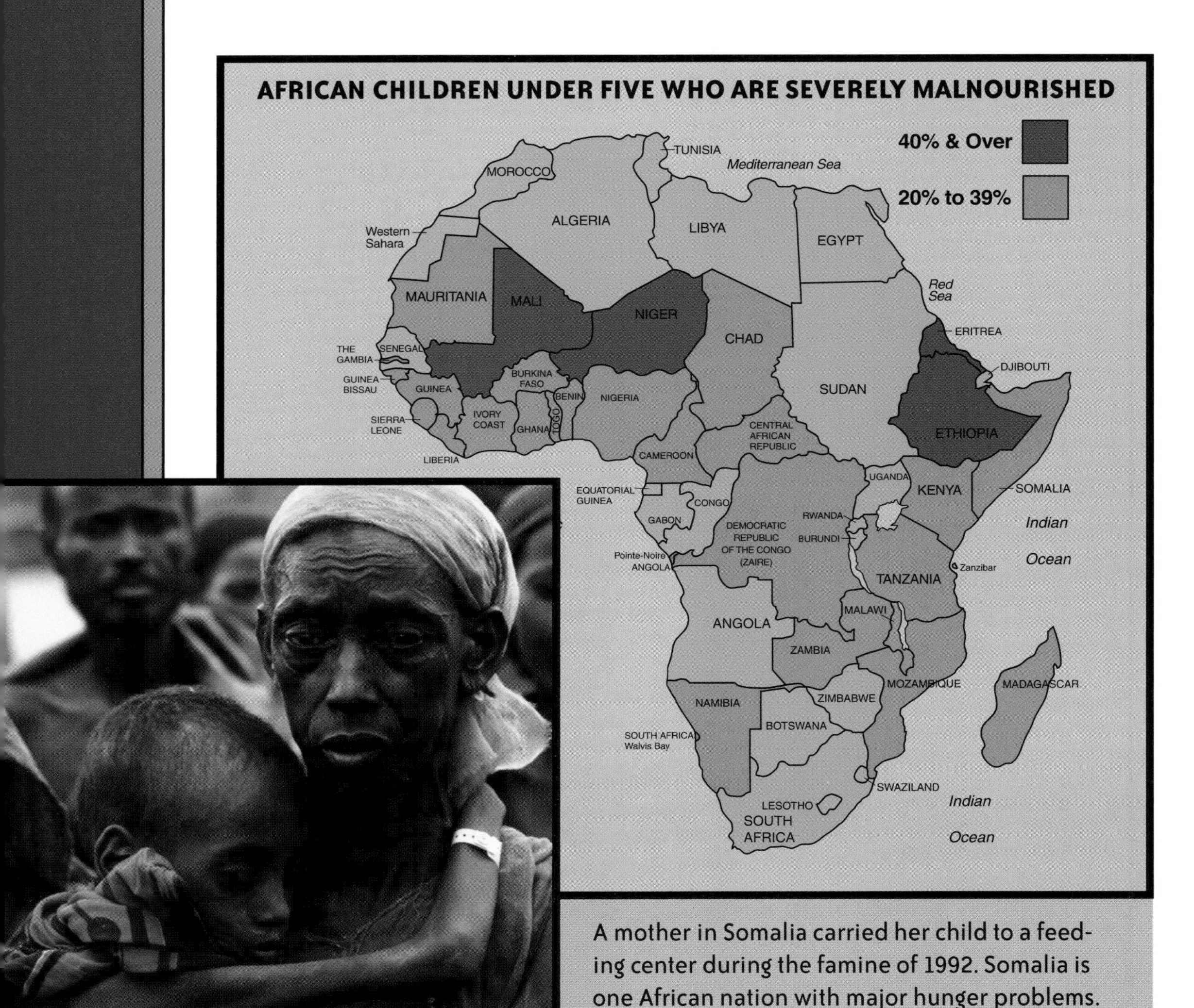

A mother in Somalia carried her child to a feeding center during the famine of 1992. Somalia is one African nation with major hunger problems.

cause of hunger and malnutrition there because it can lead to crop failures. When crops fail, food cannot be harvested. UNICEF has distributed high-protein biscuits and specially treated milk to Somali children. Similar high-protein biscuits were given to Iraqi children in 2003. War, floods, earthquakes, and hurricanes can lead to times of famine, or severe lack of food. Poverty causes many thousands of children to have little or nothing to eat. Each year, thousands of children starve to death.

Fourteen million people in the Horn of Africa spent most of 2002 in severe need of food and water. Only a year before, UNICEF and other relief organizations had worked hard to prevent a famine in that region. A famine was avoided in 2001, but about 40 percent of people living in eastern Africa are still malnourished. UNICEF has responded to this continuing emergency by supplying a high-nutrition mixture called Unimix. This mixture contains corn, beans, oil, and sugar. Children and mothers recover from malnutrition quickly when they eat Unimix regularly.

AIDS

December 1 is WORLD AIDS DAY

AIDS (acquired immunodeficiency **syndrome**) is a fatal disease that has killed millions of people worldwide since the 1980s. The disease is often transmitted from an infected mother to her unborn child. It is also spread through sexual contact or by use of an infected needle. It is first present in the blood as a virus, called HIV, for human immunodeficiency virus. Many people live a long time with HIV without coming down with the often deadly AIDS.

HIV/AIDS has spread rapidly around the world. In 2002, about 3.1 million people died of AIDS. Of this group, six hundred thousand were children. Another eight hundred thousand children became infected with HIV that year. Most of the new infections occur in sub-Saharan Africa. In that region, AIDS hurts young people in many ways. UNICEF has made a strong commitment to the HIV/AIDS challenge.

So Many Orphans

Amélia, 13, lives in Côte d'Ivoire (Ivory Coast). Her father, a police officer, died of AIDS a few years ago. She, her older sister Nadège, and their mother had to sell their house and move to a less expensive place to live. Then their mother died of AIDS. Amélia and her sister had to move to a poor area. These sisters, and many children like them, fear for their future. They must also face the fear and rejection of relatives and people in their community. In their culture, AIDS is associated with evil spirits, so AIDS victims and their families are avoided. UNICEF has started projects to help children in these circumstances. A network known as N'zrama gives these kids a place to learn the truth about the disease and talk about their feelings and experiences. Teenagers like Nadège who must act as heads of their families also get practical help. For example, the sisters received a loan to start up a firewood business. They support themselves by selling firewood on the roadside.

UNICEF's program for prevention of HIV/AIDS means educating young people about the ways AIDS is spread. Most don't know how to protect themselves. They must learn how to avoid exposure to the virus, which can be transmitted by sexual contact. Often the best teachers are **peers**, young people just like them. To help young people get the information they need to protect themselves against HIV/AIDS, UNICEF started peer discussion groups. The organization also encourages young people to take an active part in its AIDS awareness programs.

Peer support is working in Africa. However, China has no such groups for people living with HIV/AIDS. In 1999, UNICEF funds helped to produce a documentary filmed in China. The film features four HIV-positive Chinese young people who shared their personal stories. This act was a brave one because people in China do not openly discuss the disease.

North America
940,000
Caribbean
420,000
Latin America
1.4 Million
Western Europe
560,000
North Africa &
Middle East
440,000
Sub-Saharan Africa
28.1 Million
Eastern Europe
& Central Asia
1 Million
East Asia & Pacific
1 Million
South &
South-East Asia
6.1 Million
Australia
& New Zealand
15,000

UNICEF's map shows the locations of the forty million people living with AIDS at the end of 2001.

Right: UNICEF-sponsored programs around the world emphasize peer education. These young people in Zambia were part of an AIDS awareness program in 2000.

UNICEF helps purchase and distribute HIV/AIDS medications. They are sent all over the world to health care centers serving children and mothers.

Safe Water and Sanitation

Lack of clean water is a part of everyday life for millions of people in many developing countries. Diseases such as cholera and conditions such as diarrhea can result where water is dirty and sanitation is not practiced. (Sanitation includes removing human and animal waste to keep water supplies clean.)

Cholera affects the stomach and intestine. It is caused by a toxin produced by bacteria, and it can be deadly. For people who are already

These women in Bangladesh know that the area around a hand pump must be kept clean so that the water underneath the ground remains safe.

weak, a simple disorder such as diarrhea can be life threatening.

About 1.1 billion people still are deprived of safe drinking water. In most parts of the developing world, clean, unpolluted drinking water is available nearby. Plenty of **groundwater** is stored right beneath the surface of the earth, and it can be brought up by wells. All that is needed is an efficient way to bring the water to the surface. The answer is to use a hand pump. The hand pump is cheap to operate and friendly to the environment. It is an efficient way to bring clean water to people where they live.

A hand pump fits right over a village well. It does not need electricity to pump water to the surface. It is easy to repair and cheap to operate. In twenty years, the simple hand pump has given one billion people in more than forty countries plenty of safe drinking water.

Worldwide Water Watch

Every nation has its own water problems, some of which UNICEF works to cure. The 2001 earthquake in Gujarat, India, badly damaged water and sanitation systems in the area. UNICEF set up more than 3,400 tanks to store water temporarily. In Bangladesh, rainwater is used for cooking and drinking. UNICEF is helping to install rainwater collection systems in that country. In Somalia, UNICEF has dug wells, repaired latrines, or toilet facilities, and provided chlorine to kill disease-carrying bacteria. It is also helping to rebuild water systems in several cities.

March 22 is WORLD WATER DAY

In El Salvador, earthquakes in 2001 left seven hundred thousand people without water. UNICEF and its partners brought water to the people by truck. The quakes destroyed many water and sanitation systems. UNICEF provided five thousand tons of chlorine to treat wells and water systems. Other supplies include water testing kits, family-sized water jugs, and half a million water purifying tablets.

A cease-fire took place in Angola in April 2002. One significant problem remained—a lack of clean water. Millions of people were at risk for water-related diseases. UNICEF stepped in to help. The organization showed communities how to set up water cleaning systems. UNICEF provided the pipes, cement, pumps, and other materials the people needed to get their water systems started. UNICEF aid also included building latrines for schools.

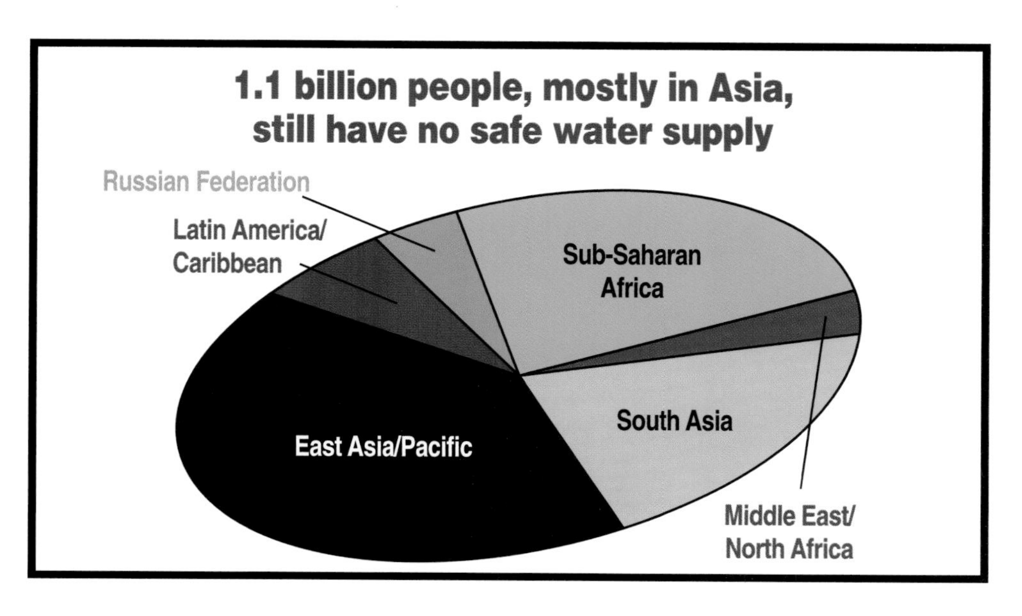

Chapter Three The Task of Education

In early 1961, President Kennedy made a speech at his inauguration in Washington, D.C. He said, "To those peoples in the huts and villages of half the globe struggling to break the bonds of mass misery, we pledge our best efforts to help them help themselves." His inspiring words marked the beginning of the "Decade of Development." The decade promised a spirit of cooperation between nations.

The Whole Child

UNICEF held a year-long study in the 1960s. The organization listened to many experts who shared interesting thoughts and ideas. The most important idea was that children are a country's most valuable natural resource. The child is not to be seen in parts—physical health, education, recreation, religion—but as a "whole child" with needs that involve family, community, nation, and planet. Children are not just small, separate bits of society; they are part of all society. Education is a human right and need of all the world's children. UNICEF recognizes that children are the future and that they need to be educated.

This boy, who lives in the West Bank, likes going to school and hopes that war won't interrupt his studies.

The New School

In the early 1970s, UNICEF began to focus on education programs for poor children in rural areas. Children in rural areas did not have the same quality of schooling as children in towns and cities. They often dropped out of school after only a year or two because they were needed to work to help their families earn a living. They couldn't stay at school all day and not work. Literacy rates, the percentage of people who

Back to School

Fatanah is a fifth-grade student in Kabul, Afghanistan. For five years, she was not allowed to attend school because the ruling Taliban was against education for girls. Fatanah had to stay inside her home and watch her brothers go off to school. Like many girls in her country, she was secretly home schooled. When the Taliban was overthrown, learning for all returned to Afghanistan.

Fatanah is thirteen years old and should be in the seventh grade. She is determined to work hard and catch up. She uses supplies given by UNICEF: pens and colored pencils, notebooks, and geometry sets. UNICEF also supplied blackboards, tents to set up temporary classrooms, and teaching and learning materials. Seven thousand tons of supplies were delivered by opening day of school, March 23, 2002.

Fatanah's father, Shah Hakim, says, "She has completely changed now. She's smiling all the time, she's no longer sick and the light has come back into her eyes. It's because she's back at school. I love when she comes back from school and tells us all about what she learned, as she used to. The dark period is over."

could read and write, were dropping. A new vision of ways to educate rural people was needed.

A successful experiment in Colombia had UNICEF's support. In Colombia's rural schools, teachers and books were in short supply. One or two teachers led children of several grades grouped together. The *Escuela Nueva* ("New School") program began in 1975. This program stressed practical skills such as reading and arithmetic. Teachers made sure the children were given knowledge that could be useful to them as members of their communities. Children learned about their history and culture and about health and nutrition.

By 1985, there were eight thousand *Escuelas Nuevas* in Colombia. UNICEF worked with the Colombian government to expand the program even more. By 1989, eighteen thousand schools had adopted the program. The rural children scored well in several subjects, especially math.

Emergency Education

Many children in Angola cannot go to school regularly. They may even stop attending completely. Because of almost constant war, about one million children have no schools to attend. If there is a school nearby, it lacks basic supplies, learning materials, and most important, good teachers. Good teachers need good training.

In January 2002, UNICEF organized training programs for one hundred schoolteachers in Angola. UNICEF also provides refresher courses for experienced teachers. Fifteen hundred teachers and assistants have been trained to bring schooling to children in refugee camps. These children who have had to abandon their homes have special needs.

UNICEF has been working with its partners to create an emergency education plan for such cases. UNICEF helped start a mini-school program for seven thousand children. The program supports reading and writing groups for twenty thousand refugee children. UNICEF has also distributed learning materials to 120,000 children.

School in a Box

Earthquakes, fires, or storms can wipe out schools overnight. Wars can send children into refugee camps far away from their schools. UNICEF believes that no matter how bad a situation is, children have the right to schooling. Since 1990, UNICEF has been supplying disaster areas with everything needed in one box to put eighty children into school. UNICEF's Copenhagen warehouse ships edukits, which have also been

These children in war-torn Angola attended school in 1998 using equipment provided by UNICEF's School in a Box program.

called School in a Box, to thousands of students every year. In 2001, nineteen thousand kits reached children in refugee camps and areas where natural disasters had struck. As the crisis situation improves, UNICEF expects the kits to be replaced by regular school materials.

The edukit supplies come in a lightweight metal storage box, which can be locked. The kit includes paint and a brush to turn the lid into a blackboard. Teachers get such items as pens, a clock, exercise books, flip charts, and posters of letters, numbers, and multiplication tables. Students gets crayons, erasers, exercise books, pencils and a pencil sharpener, carrier bags, rulers, scissors, and slates.

In early 2002, more than 780 edukits arrived in Kabul, Afghanistan. Most of the boxes were shipped into rural areas where it was hoped that many girls would be able to attend school for the first time.

Chapter Four Women and Girls

UNICEF places great value on the well-being of women. For much of its history, it has cared for mothers and their babies. The organization helps women have safer childbirths. It supports mothers who want to breast-feed their infants.

In the late 1980s, UNICEF realized that women need its support in other roles besides motherhood. Women play an important part in society, and in developing countries, they have many roles. They are educators, mothers, farmers, workers, and community leaders. Women are the heads of their households in about one-third of homes in these countries. Yet women and girls still experience inequality and abuse.

In some cultures, it is common to cut girls' bodies in their private areas, or genitals. This practice is known as female genital mutilation, or FMG. FMG has no medical reason; it is a painful act with a long history. It robs girls of their dignity and makes them ashamed to be female. Cutting their bodies this way is a form of abuse. Many people around the world are speaking out against FMG.

This little girl of Timor-Leste (East Timor) got an early education in one of the perpetual tasks women must carry out in many parts of the world—gathering firewood.

The Best Start in Life

UNICEF is concerned about the lives and health of all children from the time they are born. The organization advocates breastfeeding as the best start a child can have in life, especially for babies in developing countries where feeding babies artificial **formula** can lead to problems. Formula may be mixed with unclean water, or it can be measured incorrectly. These situations may lead to disease or malnutrition for the infant.

Introducing Meena!

In South Asia, UNICEF helped create a cartoon series to support girls in India, Bangladesh, Pakistan, and Nepal. The main character is a ten-year-old girl named Meena. With her pet parrot Mithu, Meena has adventures that teach while being funny. Meena shows girls how to think about themselves in new ways.

Prejudice against girls is strong in South Asia. The Meena series aims to change the way girls in this region are treated. This is a challenging project because the idea of girls' rights is still a new one. But the idea is catching on.

Meena is a popular program. Meena dolls, greeting cards, posters, clothing, and comic books are available. This well-loved character is even present in the school curriculum. The Meena project is a bold experiment for UNICEF and its partners. UNICEF hopes the Meena character will change the views of hundreds of millions of people.

In 1992, UNICEF and WHO started a program to create "Baby-Friendly Hospitals." To be rated as "baby-friendly," a hospital agrees not to use breastfeeding substitutes, such as formulas and bottles. Hospital staff keep the mother and her baby together as much as possible. Nurses are specially trained to help breastfeeding mothers.

A Code for Mothers and Children

The Nestlé Company once used a catchy jingle in its advertising: "N-E-S-T-L-E-S, Nestlé's makes the very best. . . ." The company makes many foods children like, such as hot chocolate mixes, cereals, and candy. It also makes artificial infant formula.

Nestlé is one of the largest infant formula makers. Such companies want to sell formula to mothers in developing countries. During the 1960s and 1970s, the companies gave hospitals free samples of their formula for newborns. Nestle hired workers to dress as nurses and bring the samples to towns and villages in rural areas. After the free samples are used up, the mother's body had stopped producing milk. The mother had to buy the formula to feed her baby.

People around the world reacted to this situation. They launched a boycott against Nestlé in 1977. (A boycott is a refusal on the part of consumers to buy any of a company's products.) The boycotters hoped Nestlé's profits would be hurt and the company would be forced to change its ways.

In 1979, UNICEF and WHO held a meeting in Geneva, Switzerland. The organizations wanted to discuss infant feeding. People from other UN agencies, spokespersons from infant food companies, and government representatives also attended. UNICEF drafted a document at this meeting in response to the Nestlé situation. The document was called the International Code on the Marketing of Breast Milk Substitutes. The code promotes breastfeeding, which helps protect children from disease. UNICEF and other nutrition experts agree that infant formula companies should not come between mothers who want to breastfeed and their babies. The companies should not put profits ahead of the health of a mother and her child.

The boycott, which had ended in 1984, was reinstated in 1988 when it became clear that Nestlé and other companies, such as Wyeth, were not following the code. The code was signed by the United States in 1994. In 1998, however, the *British Medical Journal* reported that baby formula manufacturers in general still were not following the code. The boycott continues today in at least eighty countries, including the United States.

Not all babies are born to mothers in hospitals or in places where they can get infant formula. Many babies are born to teenage girls who live on the streets of cities, where they came looking for a better way of life. UNICEF provides financial support to a number of local organizations that try to help such girls build futures.

Children in Difficulty

Chapter Five

At its founding in 1946, UNICEF's original goal was to help children in emergencies. This goal remains important today. UNICEF works to protect children from harmful situations. Emergencies of all kinds—natural disasters, wars, and diseases—threaten children all over the world. AIDS is now a health emergency, especially in Africa. Other epidemic diseases may occur after natural disasters, such as floods and earthquakes. AIDS and these other diseases are treated as emergencies. Problems in society, such as the plight of street children, are also a concern to UNICEF staff and field workers.

Natural Disasters

An event in nature that causes destruction of human life and goods is called a natural disaster. These events include floods, droughts, earthquakes, and hurricanes.

During a drought, crops may grow slowly or not at all. A poor growing season can lead to famine. Famine struck Africa when several harvests failed during the 1970s. Parts of Africa suffered a drought that lasted from 1982 to 1985.

Population growth may also be a reason for a scarce food supply. A region's food production may not keep up with the number of people to feed there.

UNICEF relief trucks arrived in Afghanistan from Pakistan in 2001. They carried children's clothing, protein mix, medicines, and educational materials.

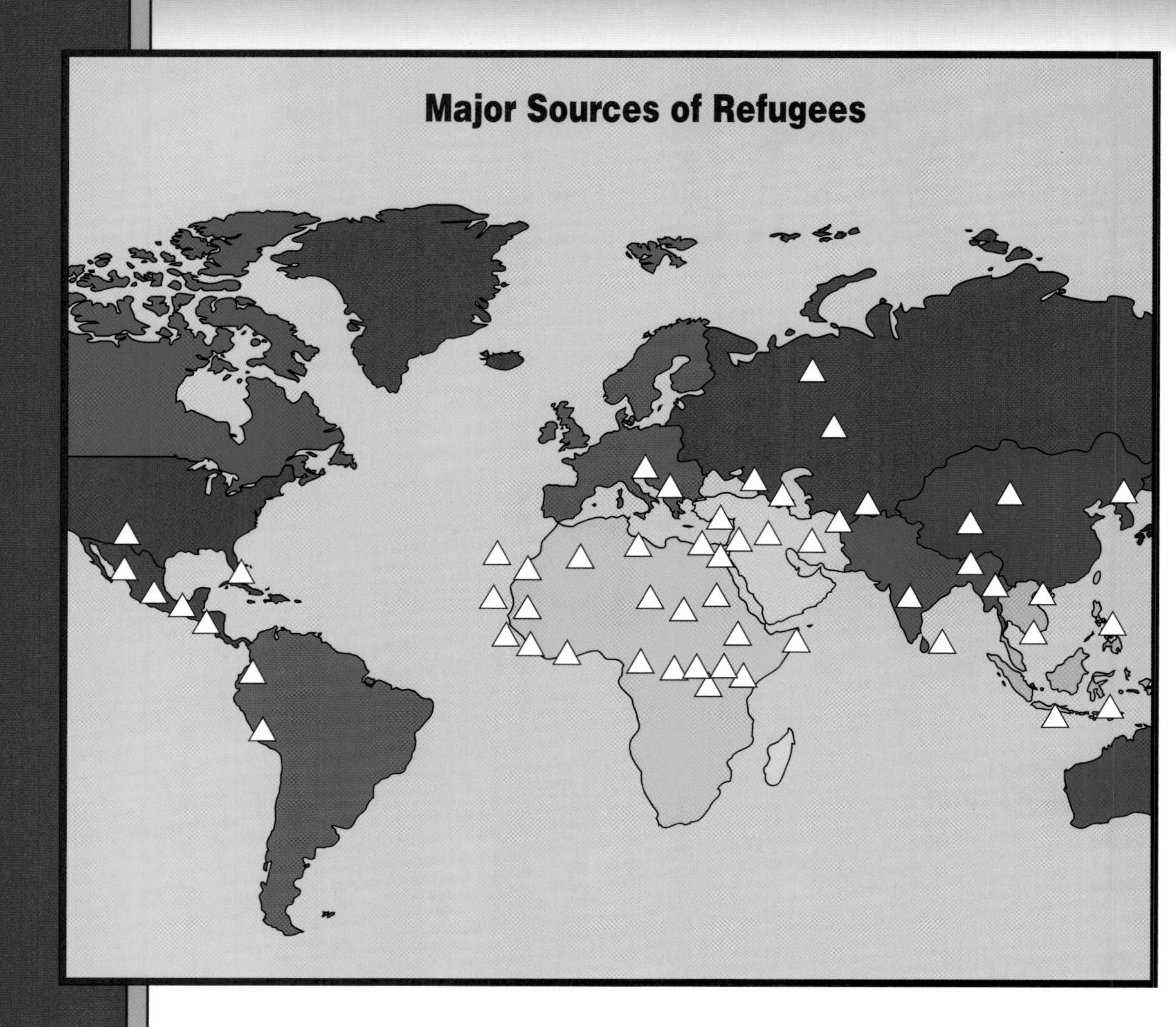

Numerous problems have occurred in sub-Saharan Africa. People flee their homes to escape famine and drought. Thousands or even millions of people move together from one region to another in a mass migration.

Depending on where they move, these people are known as either refugees or internally displaced persons (IDPs). A refugee crosses an international border to go from one country into another. Internally displaced persons do not cross a border but stay within their own country.

In 2001, a strong earthquake occurred in Gujarat, western India. It measured 7.7 on the Richter scale. This earthquake killed twenty thousand people, destroyed one million homes, and left five million children suffering. The children lost families, friends, homes, and schools—their entire way of life. UNICEF brought in survival kits for thousands of families. The kits included large plastic tents, pots and pans, and clothing. UNICEF helped the local government rebuild schools and health care centers. Six months after the quake, more than two thousand schools had opened using equipment donated by UNICEF.

IDP/Refugee Camps

People move to escape destruction and death caused by war in their lands. They seek safety or refuge. Many people crowd together in the camps. There, they hope to be safe, but a camp can become a dangerous place. There may be too many people and not enough food and clean water. Sickness may spread. Those who are fighting the war may prevent food from reaching refugees.

Internally displaced persons gathered at a feeding camp in Ethiopia after several years of drought and food shortages made it impossible for them to feed themselves.

Without UNICEF's help, the camps would be places of misery. UNICEF sends kits of special supplies to these camps. These supplies help make life for refugees easier

Child-Friendly Spaces

A refugee camp can be a scary place for a child. Life is no longer "normal." Children in refugee camps have special needs. They may have seen death and violence close up, perhaps losing parents, friends, brothers, or sisters. Their homes may have been destroyed. Children often suffer long after the event has passed. They may have nightmares and feel sad and fearful all the time.

UNICEF has set up "child-friendly spaces" for these children in crisis. The spaces are in refugee camps, such as in Turkey, where an earthquake took place. They are in places hit by war, such as Afghanistan, Albania, Chechnya, and Angola. A child-friendly space is like a safety zone where children can learn and play. UNICEF also sends counselors to help children talk about their feelings. Play can be an important part of a child's healing, and playing a sport feels "normal" to children. UNICEF provides toys and games, such as dolls, trucks, puzzles, blocks, puppets, dominoes, stuffed animals, and art supplies. The UNICEF warehouse in Copenhagen sends Recreation Kits as emergency supplies. A kit contains sports equipment for up to forty children. In 2001, UNICEF sent 2,700 Recreation Kits to children in emergency situations.

and more hopeful. When UNICEF learns of a disaster, its warehouse staff in Copenhagen, Denmark, acts quickly. The staff packs twenty-nine different kinds of kits. Each kit is meant for use in a particular situation. These kits are put together and shipped quickly to save lives. The warehouse staff prepares and ships emergency supplies within twenty-four hours. Some of these supplies include water purification tablets, vaccines and medicine, blankets, and medical equipment. In 2001, UNICEF shipped more than seventy-five thousand kits to eighty-four countries.

A Day in a Refugee Camp

Life in a refugee camp is not easy. Children may find themselves crowded into a small space with many other people. They may walk to a latrine shared by many families. They often have to be patient and wait because there are so many other people doing the same thing. They have to wait in line to collect water for washing and cooking. Clean water is scarce, so they must be careful how they use it. They may also wait in line for medical checkups and vaccinations. They even have to wait in line for meals provided by UNICEF workers.

Some children may be luckier. Perhaps they share a tent with just their own family. Perhaps their family eats together in the tent. Their family may use pots and pans and a small stove sent from the UNICEF warehouse. Each camp is different.

Refugee camps may be used for only a short time, perhaps a few weeks. Many children, however, have to live in camps for a long time, perhaps until a war is over or until new homes are built. They start to miss their own homes, their friends, even their schools. Other children are in the same situation, and they become new friends. They talk together about being sad and angry at having to stay in the camp. They are glad that UNICEF has set up a school because school helps them feel more normal. They get to play games after class, which also helps. Teachers and UNICEF workers try to make life as good as possible.

War and Land Mines

UNICEF first assisted children after World War II, and children still suffer as victims of war today. Wars create terrible problems for children and families. Land mines kill or hurt thousands of children each year. Families may have to escape war by leaving their homes behind and

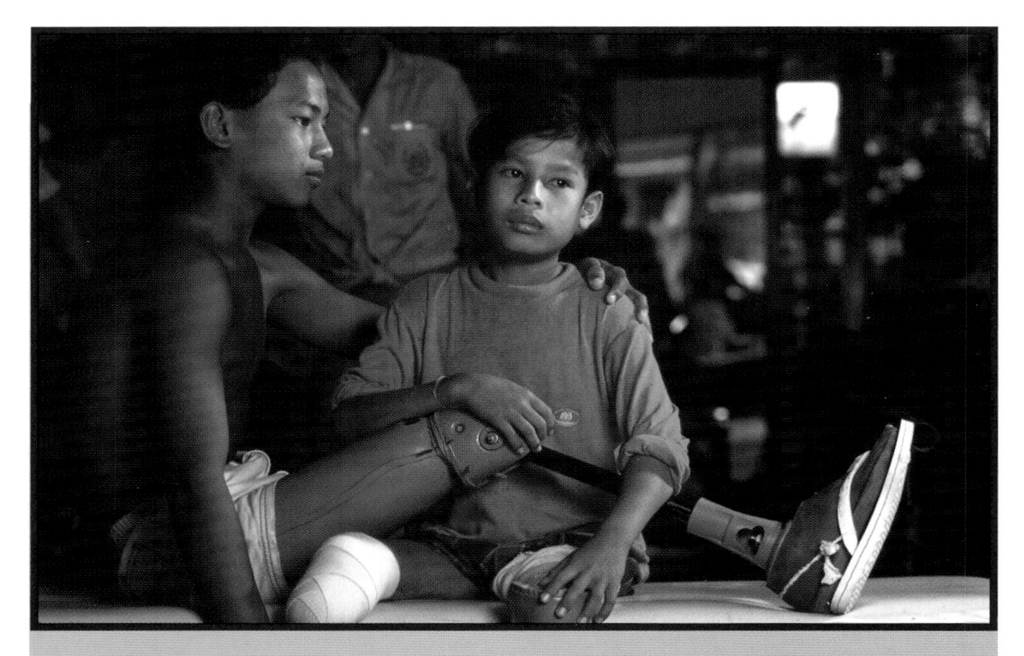

After having their feet blown off by land mines, these two young Cambodian boys learned to walk again at a rehabilitation center in 1996.

settling in a refugee or IDP camp. Boys even may be forced to help soldiers or to take part in war themselves.

A land mine is a small bomb hidden in the ground. These explosive devices buried in the land are weapons of war. During a war, thousands of mines may be buried. When a tank or other vehicle rolls over a land mine, it explodes. The vehicle is destroyed or at least damaged. When soldiers step on hidden land mines, they are badly hurt or killed. After a war ends and the soldiers leave, unexploded land mines remain behind. Children at play can step on a land mine. Sometimes a child finds a land mine and handles it. Many children have lost an arm or a leg or an eye to a land mine. Children are at high risk because they move about freely, they are close to the ground, and they are curious by nature. Women are also at risk because they gather water and firewood outdoors—usually with their children.

An estimated 110 million land mines are buried throughout sixty countries. Cambodia has seven million mines. Thousands of people there have been hurt or killed by mines. El Salvador also has many land mines remaining from a twelve-year war. UNICEF asked the Salvadoran army and government to help create mine awareness programs in schools and communities.

Afghanistan has one of the highest numbers of land mines worldwide, left behind when the Soviet Union abandoned its attempt to conquer the country in 1989. UNICEF works with the UN Mine Action Program to solve the problem. Together they have begun a training program to show people how to clear the land mines safely. With its partners, UNICEF launched a school campaign in the 1990s to make children aware of the danger of land mines. About 3,800 schools across Afghanistan participated in the campaign.

In Angola, up to ten million land mines may be hidden throughout the country. More than seventy thousand people have been hurt or killed by land mines already. UNICEF works with the Angolan government to rid the country of land mines. People in the community are specially trained by UNICEF and its partners to safely remove these mines. Land mine awareness is part of Angolan children's education.

Child Soldiers

War swept through several regions during the 1980s. In countries such as El Salvador, Uganda, Cambodia, Peru, and Ethiopia, boys in their early teens were commonly drafted as soldiers. Not all were trained to use guns to kill. They also worked as cooks and messengers. Some boys wanted to be soldiers, but others had to be forced. By 1988, there were about two hundred thousand of these boy soldiers around the world. In Sierra Leone, more than five thousand boys were separated from their families. They were forced to join the military. Half a million boys, ages twelve to eighteen, took part in the Iran-Iraq War. Thousands of these

This child soldier served in Iraq in the Gulf War of 1991. UNICEF and other organizations are trying to end such exploitation of children.

boys had a deadly job—finding land mines, and many were killed doing it. UNICEF spoke out against this practice. During a 1985-1986 vaccine drive in Uganda, a UNICEF representative met with a Ugandan Army leader to discuss the problem. UNICEF also brought the problem to the attention of the news media. This publicity helped make more people aware of the problem.

The Convention on the Rights of the Child addresses the problem. In a section on children and armed conflict, countries are offered a choice. They are asked to agree not to use children younger than 18 in the military.

Hope for Street Children

Children live on the streets for many reasons. They may be orphans and have nowhere to live. In many cases, poverty forces parents to send their children out to earn money for the family. Thousands of children in Mozambique work hard for very small wages. More than thirty thousand children work on the streets of Kabul, Afghanistan. They search for cheap things to sell, such as cigarettes from ashtrays and chewing gum. Most of the large cities in Brazil have groups of these homeless children in their streets.

The 1979 International Year of the Child was the beginning of the world's awareness of these children. UNICEF wanted to learn more about them. In 1981, Peter Taçon, a Canadian worker for UNICEF, studied the lives of street children in Brazil. His study brought these children to the world's attention. It led to UNICEF helping those groups that worked with street children. UNICEF connected the groups' efforts, which made the groups' influence stronger. UNICEF offices in places such as India, the Philippines, Kenya, and Ecuador got involved.

Today, protection of street children is part of the UNICEF "whole child" way of thinking. UNICEF continues to support grassroots, or local, groups that help street children. These groups provide meals, shelter, schooling, counseling, and sports activities. They also give children of the streets a sense of safety and family.

This child in India lives near an urban garbage dump. UNICEF supports local organizations that try to help such children and their families.

Chapter Six A New Century for Children

The first years of the twenty-first century have been important ones for children—and for UNICEF. Children's voices are being heard in new ways. UNICEF has found new partners in many different fields to help carry on its work.

UNICEF met with the world soccer governing body, FIFA (*Fédération Internationale de Football Association*), on November 20, 2001. The two groups made an official alliance, or friendly connection. This means they will work together for a common cause—children's rights. Soccer, known to most of the world as football, is the most popular sport in the world. During the World Cup games, more than one billion people watch the events. UNICEF promoted children's rights in cooperation with FIFA during the 2002 World Cup.

U.S. soccer player Brandi Chastain (center) helped promote the UNICEF-FIFA alliance. At the announcement event in 2002, UNICEF executive director Carol Bellamy stood behind the Women's World Cup star. The UN's secretary general, Kofi Annan, is shown at the right.

Along with soccer legend Pelé, fourteen-year old Alhaji from Sierra Leone attended the meeting. Alhaji spoke to the international press. "I have been a child involved in armed conflict," he said. "What we former child soldiers want most is to live a normal life—to be able to move about freely, to attend the schools of our choice, to be able to visit our friends and family . . . for our parents to be able to work to support and educate us, and to be able to play."

A World Fit for Children

We promise to create a world fit for children. We want to see long lasting human development that includes the best for every child. This human development will be based on:

- Democracy
- Equality
- Nondiscrimination
- Peace
- Social justice
- The links between all human rights, including the right to development.

We believe that together we will build a world:

- where all girls and boys can enjoy their childhood.
- where they can play and learn.
- where children are loved, respected, and cherished.
- where their rights are promoted and protected, without any kind of discrimination.
- where their safety and well-being are more important than anything else.
- where children can develop in health, peace, and dignity.

—from the "child-friendly" version, produced by Save the Children

A World Fit for Children

In May 2002, world and government leaders, child advocates, and young people met at a UN Special Session on Children. This gathering met to discuss ways the 1990 World Summit had reached its goals. They also spoke about problems that still remained. Participants wanted to develop a new plan of action to improve the lives of children and adolescents around the world over the next ten years. The document that was drawn up as a result of that 2002 meeting is called "A World Fit for Children." Some ideas expressed in that document are shown above.

Back in 1990 at the World Summit for Children, a community of nations had promised to work hard for children. This community has

"Say Yes" Ten Rallying Points for Children

Leave No Child Out
Put Children First
Care for Every Child
Fight HIV/AIDS
Stop Harming and Exploiting Children
Listen to Children
Educate Every Child
Protect Children from War
Protect the Earth for Children
Fight Poverty: Invest in Children

Left: Twelve-year-old Australian Barron Hanson led the audience in a "Say Yes for Children" rallying call celebrating the global pledge campaign during the UN Special Session on Children in 2002.

agreed to continue to work even harder until every child is safe from poverty, violence, and disease. The Global Movement is made up of individuals, government leaders, businesses, and other groups. The movement calls upon these people to find ways to give children a voice and to put children first. The "Say Yes for Children" campaign grew from the Global Movement for Children. Teachers, children, and parents around the world were asked to pledge to support ten actions that would improve the lives of children everywhere.

During the UN Special Session of May 2002, twelve-year-old Barron Hanson took part in a ceremony at UN headquarters in New York. The young delegate from Australia had come to share and listen at the Children's Forum. As the forum came to an end, Barron presented the final total of pledges gained in UNICEF's "Say Yes for Children" campaign—an amazing ninety-four million. Pledges are still coming in.

"The 21st Century Will Be More Glorious"

The Chinese government has much work to do in the area of human rights. There is still much abuse in China, particularly the practice of female infanticide. A hopeful start has been made toward recognizing the rights of children.

In 2003, UNICEF announced its new "25 by 2005" literacy plan to end, by the year 2005, differences in the education of boys and girls in twenty-five countries chosen as priorities. The campaign includes countries in Africa, Asia, and South America. Carol Bellamy says, "There can be no

These girls are unusual in Yemen because in that Middle Eastern nation, fewer than 25 percent of girls are literate. Yemen is one of the countries being targeted in UNICEF's "25 by 2005" literacy program.

significant or sustainable transformation in societies and no significant reduction in poverty until girls receive the quality basic education they need to take their rightful place as equal partners in development."

In December 1999 in Beijing, China, children celebrated the tenth anniversary of the CRC. UNICEF's partners in China marked the progress they had made together.

These are just two of the programs being carried out around the world by UNICEF for the benefit of children. Tomorrow's children in developing countries may face futures as bright as those of the children in the industrial nations of the world.

How Kids Can Help

Kids can help other kids in many ways by earning money for UNICEF. There's the "Trick-or-Treat for UNICEF" program, of course, and there are also other ways to help UNICEF year-round. Here are some suggestions:

- Have a bake sale, a car wash, a crafts sale, or a rummage sale.
- Have a talent show and charge for admission and refreshments.
- Collect bottles and cans and redeem the deposits.
- Have a pizza party. Ask a local pizzeria to donate pies and charge a bit extra per slice to raise funds for hungry children.
- Hold a raffle. Sell chances to people so they can guess the number of candies, cookies, or other treats in a large jar. The correct guess wins the jar of goodies, and the money collected helps UNICEF help kids.
- Consider skipping a snack or soda and setting aside the change for hungry kids in Africa or South Asia.
- Organize a special event, such as an auction. Local businesses can donate services such as a manicure or a year of dry cleaning. Neighbors can donate items such as antiques and collectibles such as baseball cards or Star Wars figures.
- Hold a dance-a-thon, read-a-thon, or walk-a-thon for UNICEF. Ask people to donate money for every mile walked, hour danced, or book read. Have the dance-a-thon in a school or church hall and charge for admission and refreshments.

Individuals can make donations to UNICEF by calling 1-800-FOR-KIDS or mailing a check made out to U.S. Fund for UNICEF. Send contributions to UNICEF, 333 East 38th Street, New York, New York 10016.

Time Line

1939–1945 World War II, the most destructive war in human history, is fought throughout Europe and the Pacific.

December 1946 The International Children's Emergency Fund (ICEF) is created to help children in Europe after World War II.

1950 The United Nations General Assembly votes to expand ICEF's role.

1953 ICEF becomes UNICEF, a permanent part of the United Nations.

1959 The United Nations General Assembly adopts the Declaration of the Rights of the Child.

1965 UNICEF receives the Nobel Peace Prize for "the promotion of brotherhood among nations."

1979 UNICEF declares the International Year of the Child. More than 148 countries take part.

1981 The World Health Assembly approves the International Code of Marketing of Breast Milk Substitutes to encourage breastfeeding.

1982 Top health and nutrition experts meet to create a formula known as GOBI: Growth monitoring, Oral rehydration, Breast feeding, Immunization.

1987 UNICEF study, "Adjustment with a Human Face," is released, discussing ten countries where children are endangered because of the nations' debt load.

1989 The UN General Assembly adopts the Convention on the Rights of the Child.

1990 World Summit for Children, a gathering of government leaders, takes place at UN headquarters in New York City.

1996 UNICEF supports an important study, "The Impact of Armed Conflict on Children." The study focuses on how children of the world are harmed by war.

2001 UNICEF launches the "Say Yes for Children" campaign.

2003 UNICEF announces the "25 by 2005" reading literacy for girls initiative.

Glossary

advocate a strong supporter *(noun)*, or to be a strong supporter *(verb)*
exploitation unfair use of a person or resource
formula a substitute for breast milk used to feed infants
groundwater water beneath the surface of the ground, the source of springs and wells
immunized made immune, or able to resist a disease, often by vaccination
imperative a required act or duty
integral contributing to the completeness of something
malnutrition inadequate or wrong nutrition
mosque a building used for worship in the Islamic religion
peers persons of equal age, background, or social status
ratify to give formal approval
summit a meeting of top leaders
sustainable able to be kept going without a lot of input from the outside
syndrome the collection of symptoms that indicate a specific disease
vaccine a medicine that builds immunity to a specific disease. It may be given by mouth or by an injection.

To Find Out More

BOOKS

Cameron, Sara. *Out of War: True Stories from the Front Lines of the Children's Movement for Peace in Colombia.* Scholastic, 2001.

Castle, Caroline. *For Every Child: The Rights of the Child in Words and Pictures.* Phyllis Fogelman Books, 2000.

Kindersley, Anabel. *Children Just Like Me.* Dorling Kindersley, 1995.

State of the World's Children, Annual Report of UNICEF.

ADDRESSES AND WEB SITES

UNICEF
UNICEF House
3 United Nations Plaza
New York, New York 10017
U.S.A.

UNICEF
Palais des Nations
1211 Genève 10
Switzerland

www.unicef.org

This site features a complete history of UNICEF. A "Voices of Youth" page gives young people a place to share their thoughts with peers and do learning activities.

UNICEF in Mexico
www.unicef.org/mexico/
This site provides information in Spanish about UNICEF programs in Mexico.

United States Fund for UNICEF
333 East 38th Street
New York, New York 10016
www.unicefusa.org
At this site, you can read about current emergencies around the world and how UNICEF is helping.

Index